NANCY WILLARD

The Mouse, the Cat, and Grandmother's Hat

Illustrated by
JENNY MATTHESON

Little, Brown and Company
Boston New York London

This is
Grandmother's hat.

This is the mouse that hid
under Grandmother's hat.

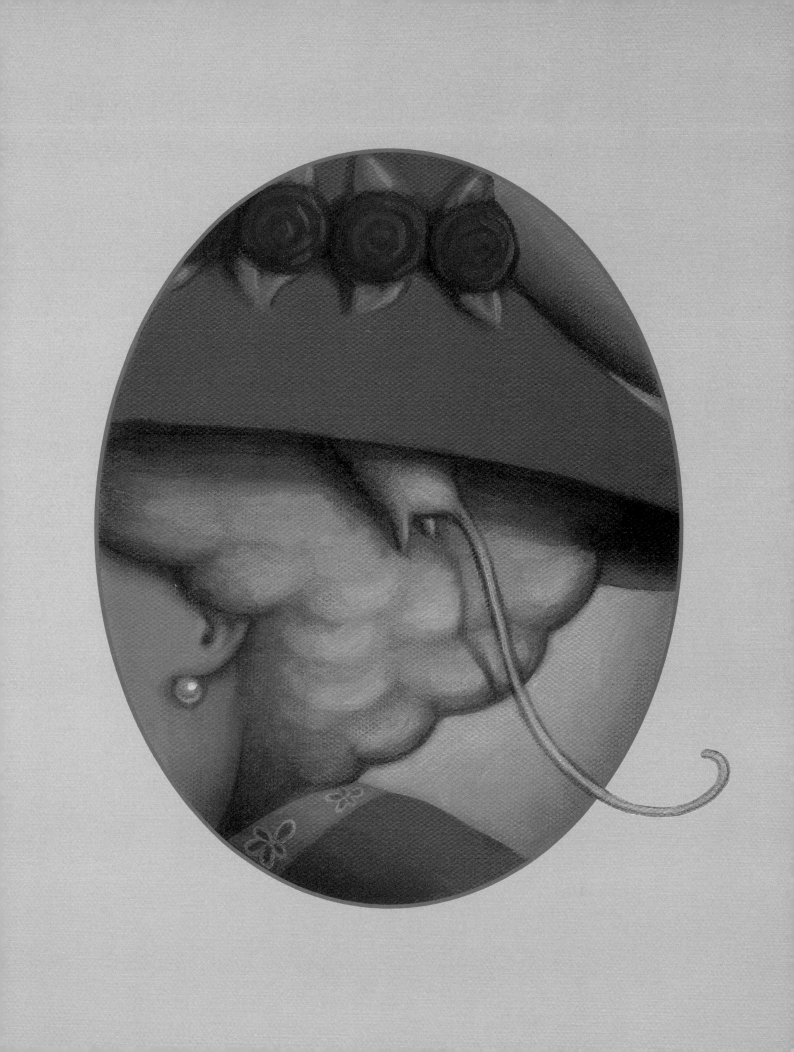

This is the cat . . .

that waits to be fed,
that mewed for the mouse
that tried to play dead
under Grandmother's hat.

This is the cake,
a birthday surprise.

This is my grandmother,
shutting her eyes.

These are the relatives,
ready to sing.

This is the mouse
with a tail like a string
under Grandmother's hat.

"Happy birthday to you!"

This is the mouse that tickled my shoe
as I carried the cake that jiggled and bounced

when the hungry cat gave a yowl and pounced.

This is the cake that sprang to the floor

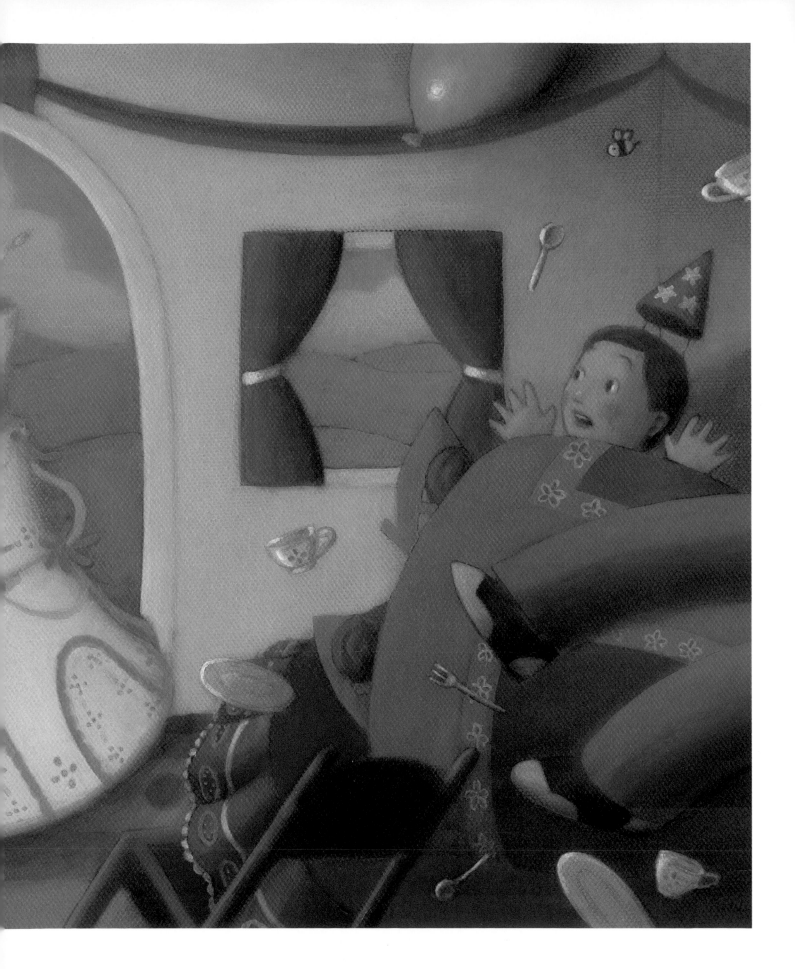

and picked itself up and rolled out the door.

This is the mouse

that didn't get caught.

These are the relatives,

shocked and distraught.

"The cake has run off!"

"Things couldn't be worse!"

I hear a bee
in Grandmother's purse.

For Maria, who met the mouse
— N. W.

To my family, my cats,
and my grandmother
— J. M.

First Edition

Library of Congress Cataloging-in-Publication Data
Willard, Nancy.
  The mouse, the cat, and Grandmother's hat / by Nancy Willard ; illustrated by Jenny
Mattheson — 1st ed.
    p. cm.
  Summary: A mouse hiding under Grandmother's hat causes quite a commotion at
her surprise birthday party.
  ISBN 0-316-94006-2
    [1. Birthdays — Fiction. 2. Parties — Fiction. 3. Grandmothers — Fiction. 4. Mice
— Fiction. 5. Stories in rhyme.] I. Mattheson, Jenny, ill. II. Title.
PZ8.3.W668 Mo 2002
[E] — dc21   00-067796

10 9 8 7 6 5 4 3 2 1

TWP

Printed in Singapore

The illustrations for this book were done in oils on canvas.
The text was set in Else, and the display type is Fontesque.